HOCKEY LUCK

Irene Punt

illustrations by
Gary O'Brien

Scholastic Canada Ltd.
Toronto New York London Auckland Sydney
Mexico City New Delhi Hong Kong Buenos Aires

Scholastic Canada Ltd.
604 King Street West, Toronto, Ontario M5V 1E1, Canada

Scholastic Inc.
557 Broadway, New York, NY 10012, USA

Scholastic Australia Pty Limited
PO Box 579, Gosford, NSW 2250, Australia

Scholastic New Zealand Limited
Private Bag 94407, Botany, Manukau 2163, New Zealand

Scholastic Children's Books
Euston House, 24 Eversholt Street, London NW1 1DB, UK

www.scholastic.ca

Library and Archives Canada Cataloguing in Publication
Punt, Irene, 1955-, author
Hockey luck / Irene Punt ; illustrated by Gary O'Brien.
ISBN 978-1-4431-4278-6 (pbk.)
I. O'Brien, Gary J., illustrator II. Title.
PS8581.U56H6 2015   jC813'.54   C2015-901865-X

6 5 4 3 2 1   Printed in Canada 121   15 16 17 18 19

MIX
Paper from
responsible sources
FSC® C004071

Contents

For Jackie Bevis. I am lucky to have such a good friend.

— I. P.

Hawks' Luck

Tom sat on the wooden bench in the dressing room at Centennial Arena. His hair was wet. His throat was dry. His face was hot. His feet were cold. "I love hockey!" he announced, slapping high-fives with his best friends, Stuart, Mark, Jordan and Harty. "What a game!"

"Yup! It's a fun day Sunday! We put two eggs in the nest!" said Mark. He flapped his arms and squawked, *"Tweet, tweet!"*

Everyone cracked up.

I love being a Hawk, thought Tom. It

was his third year playing hockey on the Glenlake Hawks. This season he and his friends moved up to the Novice Three team. Coach Howie was their coach. Yellow and green were their team colours.

Tom gazed around at his teammates. Everyone was smiling. Everyone had a wet "sweat head." It was early October and the start of a new season, but some things never changed. And that felt good. Only one thing could have made the game better for Tom . . . getting his first goal of the season.

"PSST. We won our game because I stuck NHL Band-Aids on my blisters," said Stuart proudly. "They always bring me good luck." He flashed a toothy smile.

"I eat lucky pizza on game day," said Mark. "Because a pizza that's cheesy makes scoring easy!" He reached into his hockey bag and found a slice of pepperoni pizza left over from breakfast. "I am not joking, guys. If I eat pizza, I get a goal. It's like magic!"

"I get dressed in a special order for good luck," added Harty. He explained his routine: "I put on my elbow pads first, jock second and gloves last. Then, I tuck the left side of my jersey into my hockey pants — just like Wayne Gretzky did."

"Nope," Jordan shook his head. "We won because I wore my stinkiest socks. I hide them in my goalie helmet so they never get washed." He pulled off his goalie skates. "Smell these! Once they were white and now they are bluish grey brown!"

Tom listened to his friends talk about their hockey superstitions and good luck charms. Without his lucky number 15 jersey, he needed to tell himself, *These guys are crazy. Good luck stuff is silly. There is no such thing as HOCKEY LUCK!*

Everyone in the room was showing off their weird ideas about luck. "I sing *Happy Birthday* when I tighten my skates." "I wear red underwear." "I pinch myself before going on the ice." "One time I ate three mini pizzas and got a hat trick!"

"Oh, NO!" Suddenly, Mark leapt across the room to where the hockey sticks were propped up in the corner. "TOUCH WOOD!"

he called out. "Quick! Knock on wood! Before you jinx your good luck by bragging about it!"

The team followed Mark's instructions because nobody wanted to jinx their luck. "Touch wood!" they chorused, knocking on the bench, and knocking on their heads. *RAP! RAP! RAP!* Tom shut his eyes. Deep down, he respected hockey superstitions.

He knew good luck charms were important. Lots of players in the NHL had them. *When you own something lucky, you remember all the times it brought you good hockey luck. And when you own something unlucky . . .* His heart sank. Tom pulled off his new home jersey — number 5. He frowned at the problem and stuffed it into his hockey bag.

Number 5

Coach Howie entered the dressing room. "Hawks, you are the luckiest team on the planet!" he announced. "I've never seen anything like it. Tied at 1–1 in the last minute of the game and the goalie sneezes just as Mark takes a shot!" Coach Howie wiped his forehead. "Good thing I wore my lucky cap!"

Mark looked smug. "I say . . . pizza with cheese made the toughest goalie in the league . . . sneeze! And I got a goal!"

"We *are* on a lucky streak. Remember last week? We won when the Sharks scored on

7

their own goalie!" Jordan grinned. "It was like winning the lottery!"

"And what about that crazy bounce off the top of the net?" asked Harty. "We *blooped* and . . . we scored!"

The room exploded with laughter.

Coach Howie stood on the bench. "Okay, Hawks. Settle down! I'm worried our luck will run out. We can't count on fluky goals to win! Let's get back to the basics of good hockey: using skills and executing plays." He clapped and gave a thumbs-up. "Great win today! Our next game is Wednesday at 6:30."

Mark winked at his friends as if to say, "No worries, my luck is golden. We can count on pizza!"

Tom looked like a melting snowman. His arms drooped

and his head hung low. He liked Coach Howie and, more than anything, he loved it when Coach Howie gave *him* a thumbs-up. Lately, Tom felt like everything he did was thumbs-down.

"What's up?" Harty gave Tom a friendly nudge.

"All this talk about superstitions and lucky goals makes me remember that I've lost my luck." Tom sighed. "I have . . . no lucky food, no lucky way to get dressed, no lucky socks, cap or Band-Aids. What kind of hockey player am I?"

"Oh, yeah," agreed Stuart. "Ask anyone. The best hockey players in the world have good luck charms. So do their fans and coaches."

The more Tom heard, the worse he felt. "I haven't scored a goal since last season, when I wore my old number 15 jersey. I used to say 'Go, Hawks, go!' as I pulled it over my head." Tom grunted in frustration. "This year I got dumb number 5. When we moved up to Team Three, my number 15 jersey stayed behind. Why can't Team Three have a number 15?"

"Glenlake teams don't have every number in the world," mumbled Jordan. "If they did, I'd take number 32 like Jonathan Quick."

"I like number 66," said Harty.

"Remember what Coach Howie told us? Don't put hockey skates without skate guards in your hockey bag." Stuart shivered. "Maybe some kid's blades slashed that jersey to shreds."

Tom bent over to reach into his bag. *Ripppp!* His padded hockey pants split open. When he stood up, he bumped his head. "Oh, boy!" grumbled Tom. "Besides losing my good luck, I have found bad luck!"

Mark did not laugh. He looked at Tom as if

to say, "You're right! You've got big time bad luck!"

The boys pulled their big hockey bags down the long hallway beneath the bleachers. They stopped by the spectator glass and checked out the new game on the ice. Novice Four teams were playing. Tom's eyes quickly picked out Glenlake number 15. "Hey, that girl is wearing my old jersey!"

Tom watched the play. Number 15 blazed the ice, stickhandled the puck like a pro, and then swooped to the right of the goalie and hammered a shot into the net. Goal!

Tom's heart sank. His old jersey had just worked its magic!

Sharing Luck

Mark gawked. "Man, oh man! Number 15 *is* a lucky jersey! Now that girl's got your luck! She's got *your* wicked slapshot, and she's scoring *your* goals." Mark patted Tom's shoulder. "Bummer. 'Cause you don't jive ... wearing number 5!"

The truth was painful for Tom. He yanked his hockey bag. One wheel fell off. He dragged himself and his broken bag through the doorway.

"Tom! Over here!" shouted his mom, waiting with the other parents near the snack bar. "Hurry up!" She tightened her yellow and green scarf.

Tom looked around. All Hawks parents, grandparents and fans were wearing the team colours. All for good luck and team spirit. Everybody had helped the Hawks win, except him.

Tom carried his bag down the front stairs and into the parking lot. His friends walked a few steps behind, whispering.

Just before getting into his car, Harty called out, "Hey, guys . . . how about road hockey at my house! Three o'clock!"

"Okay," said Tom, brightening. He loved road hockey almost as much as ice hockey. And there were no jerseys for road hockey, and no numbers. He'd get a goal for sure. No problem.

It was after three
o'clock. Tom
stick-handled
a tennis ball
down his
driveway and
along the sidewalk
toward Harty's house.
TAP, TAP, TAP. He concentrated on
keeping his head up and grip loose. He
looked ahead, pretending the light pole was
the goal. He took a shot. *SWOOSH!* The
ball missed the pole and bounced along
the curb — *BOING, BOING, BOING* —
stopping beneath Mrs. Corbet's car. *What
next?*

Tom shouldered his stick and picked up
his pace.

A hockey net was set up and ready on
Harty's driveway, but Tom's friends were

nowhere in sight. *Did they say two o'clock or three o'clock? Did I miss the game?* worried Tom.

As Tom neared, he could see Harty's garage door was open. His four friends were sitting at a round table. It looked like they were writing a spelling test. "We're in here!" called Harty.

"What's up?" Tom scrunched his face, feeling clued out.

"We are a team and we have a team problem," said Jordan in a nervous robot voice.

"Huh?" said Tom. His friends were acting weird. They made him feel like he was inside the principal's office.

Mark looked at the floor and spoke quickly, "You got the most goals last year. But this season . . . you are in a slump. And a funk. You need to dump the slump and fix the funk. And we are going to help you!" He let out a big breath. "Phew. I'm done."

Tom's face reddened. He knew how rotten his hockey was, but it didn't feel good to be insulted.

Mark jabbed Stuart and whispered, "Your turn."

"Tom. Um . . . First of all, you need some

luck," Stuart said sincerely. "I'm used to tripping and crashing into stuff. But, that's not you! You are our *star*. The team counts on your goals."

"You are the guy who usually helps us!" said Harty. "Now it's our turn to help you."

The four friends put their fists together and yelled, "Tom's the best!"

Tom's spirits lifted. His friends were trying their hardest. He wondered, *Can my friends really help me become lucky again?*

"We have a plan," said Harty.

Stuart passed Tom an NHL Band-Aid. "I'm sharing my secret weapons with you."

Mark pulled a handful of mushroom pizza out of his pocket. "It's a bit mushy, but it's still a goal-getter. Just eat it and see!"

Jordan held out a bag full of broccoli. "You can grow stinky socks quickly if you stuff these into the sock toes."

Tom said, "Thanks, guys." But he was still concerned. "Luck doesn't come easily."

Harty held up his mom's tablet. "I've got something that might help." Harty opened the cover. "I usually use this to look up the big words my mom uses. But we have something BIGGER to look up today! Like . . . what the NHL pros do for good luck." Harty touched the screen, concentrating on typing the words "NHL lucky charms" into the search bar.

"Okay," said Tom. He crossed his fingers. Maybe, just maybe, his friends and the entire NHL could help him find something to improve his luck.

NHL Luck

"Listen to this," said Harty, as he moved his fingers up and down the screen. "A good luck charm is 'something believed to bring good luck.'"

"Like, duh?" said Mark. "We need to know what the SOMETHING is! Like, if you paint your toenails on game day, you'll have powerful luck." He stomped his foot. "That's the kind of simple answer we're looking for!"

Stuart typed new words into the search bar: "NHL hockey superstitions." Within seconds, a list appeared.

Mark tapped on the first answer. "The Detroit Red Wings' fans throw octopuses onto the ice for good luck!"

"Cool!" they chorused, flailing their arms like a wiggly octopus.

"The Florida Panthers' fans have thrown rats on the ice in hopes of getting a *rat trick*!" Stuart read. "I hate rats."

"Those superstitions are no good for Tom. He's a Hawk on the ice, not a fan in the stands!" said Mark. "What else?"

The tablet was passed around.

"I found a good one," said Harty. "NHL forward Bruce Gardiner used to dunk his stick in the toilet, wanting to show the stick who the boss was. He gave it a good flushing." Harty's eyes widened. "We've got a bathroom just inside the door. Let's go!"

Tom grabbed his stick. The boys headed to the bathroom, sounding like a bunch of owls. "Oooo." "Oooo." "Oooo." "This is going to be goooood!"

"Now, put the blade in the water!" Harty said to Tom, pointing to the bowl.

"Then swish it around!" said Jordan. "You are the boss! You rule!"

Tom followed along.

Stuart pressed down on the flush handle. *FLUSHHH!* The water swirled up to the toilet brim and then circled down the bowl and into the drain.

"Yes!" gasped the boys. "Cool!"

Harty's sister, Wendy, crept up behind Tom. "I'm telling my mom and you are in big trouble!" she exclaimed. "MO-OM! Tom is breaking our toilet! Come quick!"

Instantly, Harty's mom appeared. She stood in the doorway, arms crossed. "What on earth are you guys doing? Get that stick out of my toilet right now! If you want to play in the toilet, I will give you each a pair of rubber gloves and a cleaning brush!"

Tom's jaw was hanging open as they ran back to the garage. "I thought I was a dead duck," he cried.

"What now?" asked Stuart.

"Sidney Crosby eats a peanut butter and jelly sandwich before his games," said Harty. "I can make you one."

"Whoa! I don't like jelly," sighed Tom.

Mark scratched his head and grabbed the tablet. He searched more websites. "I found another good one!" he said. "There was a New York Ranger known as Gratoony the Loony who used to stand on his head before a game." Mark raised his eyebrows at Tom. "Wanna try it?"

Tom nodded in desperation.

Stuart organized a pile of sleeping bags, life jackets and tarps against the garage wall. "These will be your crash pad . . . just in case. SAFETY FIRST!"

Tom squatted down. He put his hands on the floor and his head between his hands. Harty and Jordan helped pull Tom's feet and legs up.

"No! No! I'm going to fall!" cried Tom. Jordan and Harty quickly pulled him into a handstand. "Ouch! My hands! My head! My back! Ouch! Oooo. Eyeee. Aaahoooh!"

"You should put Tom down," Stuart said. "His face is purple."

THUMP! Tom flopped onto the crash pads. "Aaahoooh!" he gave one last howl.

"What's going on in there?" yelled Harty's mom, hearing the commotion. "There will be *consequences* if you break something!"

"Told you about the big words. Let's play road hockey," said Harty, waving his friends outside.

Testing Luck

Tom's pockets were filled with broccoli and pizza. He stuck the NHL Band-Aid across his chin. "I'm ready to test my luck with this stuff!" Tom gave a goofy grin, fastened his helmet and then tripped on Stuart's foot. He slowly got to his feet.

The plastic puck passed from player to player. Forward, back and across the driveway. Jordan crouched in net, making his scary goalie face. *BAM! BAM! BAM!* Jordan stopped shot after shot. Tom went for the rebound each time, and each time he missed.

Tom made perfect stick to stick passes, allowing Harty to score twice.

Five minutes later, Tom picked up a pass from Mark. He ran down the left side of the driveway, on a breakaway. *I got it. This is it*, thought Tom, eyeing Jordan, blocking the left. Tom took a shot, high and right. Jordan stopped the puck with his goalie glove.

Stuart swooped in for the rebound. He gently tapped the puck. It skipped between Jordan's big leg pads. "Goal!" squealed Stuart, dancing.

Tom dragged his feet. "How'd you do that?"

"Got lucky," said Stuart.

"*Shhh!*" Harty made a face at Stuart.

"Sorry, Tom. I forgot. I'm not supposed to mention our good luck to you," said Stuart. "It only makes you feel worse. But . . . the fact is . . . Jordan is the best goalie in the world, wearing the stinkiest socks in the

world. That is why you can't score. You don't have a chance. I usually can't score, but my NHL Band-Aids are extremely lucky."

Tom pointed to the NHL Band-Aid on his chin. "This is not lucky . . . on me! Pizza in my pocket didn't work either. And the headstand gave me a sore neck."

"You want me to take off my socks?" asked Jordan. "You can try them."

"No!" gasped Tom, choking at the suggestion.

Jordan clapped. "I've got one more idea. Start talking to the net. That's what Patrick Roy, the goalie, did during NHL games."

Tom's hopes were fading. *Is it time to give up?* he wondered. But his friends continued to look optimistic.

"Be firm!" "You're the boss!" "You rule!" they coached.

Tom took in a big breath. *No! I am not a*

quitter. No one likes a quitter. He held the orange plastic puck in his hand. In a stern voice, he said, "Listen up, net. This puck is going to hit you like a bullet, so get ready. I am getting the next goal today! Got it?"

"Good!" raved Harty.

"Now tap the posts with your stick," said Jordan.

Tom tapped the posts three times. He showed them who the boss was. Then he kissed the puck and said nicely, "Come on, plastic puck, be my buddy. Let's get a goal, just you and me."

But Tom did not score. He tripped over a tree branch and lost his shoe in a bush.

Tom plodded home. He'd had enough bad hockey for one day.

Back to Basics

It was Monday morning. The schoolyard was in chaos. Tom met his friends by the swings.

"I had nightmares all night," Tom told them. "Unlucky 5s were everywhere. The Hawks got five five-minute penalties. We got five goals against us. We had five players away. I got a nickel for my allowance. And I had a toothache! It was my worst nightmare yet."

"Yeah," said Mark. "I had a nightmare, too. Your bad luck rubbed off on us."

"No way," said Tom. But, he was worried.

What if my bad luck is contagious? It was time to try something different.

"Coach Howie always says, 'Stick to the basics. Go back to square one if you are stuck in a rut.' Maybe it's time to go back to old-fashioned superstitions," suggested Tom.

The boys began to shout out every superstition they'd ever heard. "Don't step on a sidewalk crack!" "Don't let a black cat cross your path." "Cross your fingers." "Cross your toes." "Get a horseshoe." "Pinch yourself." "Find a four-leaf clover." "Find a penny, pick it up . . ."

"Canada doesn't have pennies any more," said Tom.

"I bet our old teacher, Mrs. Wong, has one. She has everything," said Jordan.

The boys ran to her classroom door and knocked on it.

Mrs. Wong was putting up a bulletin board

display for Thanksgiving. "Hello there!" she said, greeting them with a smile. "I really miss you guys. How are the Hawks doing?"

"Tom has lost his luck in hockey. It all started when he got his new jersey," said Stuart, "and lost his lucky number 15."

"Oh dear," said Mrs. Wong, shaking her head. "Hockey players have many superstitions. I remember when my brother said the word *shutout* before a big game. His team lost 9–0. I think he talked himself out of winning! He thought they'd lose and they did." She continued, "Then he kissed the Stanley Cup when it was at the public library, and his team won their next game!"

"Wow!" exclaimed Tom.

"Do you have a lucky penny?" asked Mark. "Tom could *kiss* it for good luck!"

"Good thinking! But I haven't found a lucky penny in a long time," sighed Mrs. Wong.

The boys looked deflated.

"Hmm . . . Let's just think," suggested Mrs. Wong, walking toward her desk.

She opened the bottom drawer and fished out an old calendar. "Here, Tom. Remember when we studied English proverbs and wise sayings? I was lucky to find 365 of them in this calendar! Proverbs are full of advice. Maybe you'll find one about good fortune and luck."

Tom liked Mrs. Wong. He missed having

her as his teacher, even though he liked his new teacher, Miss Lucy.

BUZZZ! BUZZZ! The nine o'clock bell blasted.

"Don't be late for class!" said Mrs. Wong. "Remember . . . most of the time, we make our own luck!"

"Thank you," said Tom, waving goodbye. He hurried toward room number seven, carefully carrying 365 proverbs.

Making Lists

"Good morning, student geniuses," said Miss Lucy. She liked to call them important names. "Today you have a fun writing assignment! It will give you a chance to share something you know lots about." Miss Lucy hummed as she wrote the assignment on the board:

Write a list.
The title should start with:
"HOW TO_____"

Tom scratched his head. The only thing he liked to write about was hockey. "Does anyone want to share their idea?" asked Miss Lucy.

Jordan scuffed his feet under his desk.

"I'm going to write 'How to have a lemonade stand,'" said Laura. "There are lots of things to do, like make lemonade, get cups and paint a sign."

"I'm going to write 'How to become an author,'" said Kylie. "There are three easy steps."

"Excellent," said Miss Lucy. "You *can* do it, people! I smell brilliance in this classroom!" Miss Lucy had a way of making everything seem possible and everyone feel smart. "Go brains, go!" she cheered. "See if you can get twenty things on your list!"

Tom kept thinking. *I can't write "How to score a goal" because . . . I don't score any more! I HAVE BAD HOCKEY LUCK!*

He held the calendar from Mrs. Wong. He opened it and read:

"Birds of a feather flock together." Tom nodded.

"Practice makes perfect." Tom nodded.

"The best way to have good luck is to stay away from bad luck."

Tom couldn't believe it. Even the calendar knew about hockey and how to solve luck problems. Suddenly, the proverb gave Tom an idea. He opened his journal and wrote:

How to have BAD hockey luck

1. Wear number 5 on your jersey.
2. Do not practise.
3. Be late.
4. Don't listen to your coach.
5. Fool around.
6. Eat lots of candy.
7. Be tired.
8. Forget your skates.
9. Forget to sharpen your skates.
10. Go to the wrong arena.
11. Forget your mouthguard.
12. Do not follow the rules.
13. Be crabby.
14. Make fun of your team.
15. Never say thank you to the parent helpers and coach.
16. Lose your lucky number . . . (especially to a girl who wears pink ribbons).
17. Be weird.
18. Pick your nose.
19. Bring your pet snake to the game.
20. Wear number 5 on your jersey!!!!!!!

Tom read his list. It was a beauty. It made him smile inside.

Miss Lucy strolled around the classroom telling kids how amazing they were. Even Jordan, who hated writing, was busy writing a long list: "How to build an outdoor rink."

Tom thought about his week. It didn't feel good to be crabby. He picked up his pencil and wrote a new journal entry. This one was easy peasy.

How to have GOOD hockey luck

1. Listen to your coach.
2. Practise.
3. Eat healthy food.
4. Be on time.
5. Drink water.
6. Get a good night's sleep.
7. Check your equipment bag so you don't forget your gear.
8. Get your skates sharpened.
9. Go to the correct arena.

10. Check the schedule!
11. Wear your mouthguard.
12. Follow the rules.
13. Be a team player.
14. Be happy!
15. Thank the coach and parent helpers.
16. Brush your teeth.
17. Don't pick your nose.
18. Leave your pet snake at home.
19. If you have to wear a number 5 jersey, try your best anyway.
20. Stay positive . . . (even if a girl with pink ribbons gets to wear your lucky number 15 jersey).

Tom thought about Mrs. Wong's words: "You make your own luck." Sometimes she had weird ideas. But the proverb calendar was a good idea today. Tom read it one more time, this time with a few extra words:

"The best way to have good hockey luck is to stay away from bad hockey luck."

Hard Work

On Tuesday morning, Tom sat at the kitchen table finishing spelling homework. Mom rushed back and forth making breakfast and doing laundry while Dad packed lunches. The toast burned, the coffee spilled and the smoke detector went off.

"Ewww!" Mom scowled as she picked something gooey out of Tom's jeans pocket. "This is disgusting!"

"That's Mark's lucky hockey pizza," said Tom. "I was supposed to eat it to improve my hockey luck."

Mom rolled her eyes. "That Mark is a real joker."

"No, Mom. When Mark eats pizza on game day, he scores a goal," said Tom. "Don't *you* believe in hockey superstitions?"

"Well . . . the scientist in me says, NO! Superstitions are ridiculous. If Mark got a goal, it's because he deserved it, not because he downed a pizza," Mom said.

Tom frowned. "But . . . but . . . Dad has hockey superstitions. He didn't shave and the Flames won!"

Mom sighed, "Well . . . I guess . . . some lucky charms might give you *hope*. Some superstitions might make you *focus*. Having hope and focusing are good things. But you SHOULD NOT count on luck alone." She raised her finger. "Work hard and your luck will work!"

"I *have* been working hard at hockey,"

Tom sighed. "But I haven't scored a goal this season."

"Keep at it," said Dad. "Lazybones never find luck."

Phsshhh-splash-whoosh noises came from the washing machine, which was overflowing. Mom ran to hit the off button. "That's it!" She took off her blue sweater. "Every time I wear this thing, my day is a disaster!"

Dad whispered to Tom, "You'll know when you find your luck. It will hit you like a red goal light."

It was an ordinary day at school. There was journal writing, two pages of math problems and a lesson about the Bow River. Mark yawned most of the afternoon. Then he made a big discovery. If you add the letter K to Miss Lucy's name, it becomes Miss Lucky. He passed Tom a note to tell him.

Miss Lucy stood by Tom's desk. She could read the note over Tom's shoulder.

Tom shuddered. Luckily, Miss Lucy didn't get mad. Instead she said, "How's your hockey luck doing?"

"Not good," Tom mumbled. He hadn't scored at recess when playing ball hockey. Every time he passed the ball, it ended up a goal for someone else. "All the kids are good at ball hockey now, so I need to be better."

"I liked your writing assignment about hockey luck," said Miss Lucy. "Hang in there!"

"Thanks," said Tom. Miss Lucy was nice.

Kylie sat across from Tom. She leaned over and said, "If you want to be lucky, you need to be Irish. I can teach you the Irish jig."

Tom choked.

"Or the Irish sword dance," said Kylie.

"Hey, Tom," said Mark, making a face. "Swords are cool. But you might have to wear a green leprechaun suit to have the luck of the Irish."

"Get a grip! Hockey players don't wear leprechaun suits," groaned Jordan, rolling his eyes. "They wear padded pants."

Passing the Puck

School was over. Tom grabbed his backpack and headed for the crosswalk. His dad was waiting for him in his truck, parked by the lane.

"Over here!" yelled Dad, waving a box of doughnut holes. Tom ran to meet him.

"Let's go to the hockey store," said Dad. "I tried to fix the rip in your hockey pants, but it was impossible. Duct tape won't stick. And I jammed up the sewing machine with black thread. Those pants are worn out and too small anyway." Dad smiled. "Time to buy you some new ones."

"Yes!" cheered Tom, downing a doughnut hole. *New pants!* His old ones were bought at a garage sale.

Dad tuned in the local *Hockey Talk* program on the car radio.

"Today we are talking about how lucky our city is to have Junior A hockey players who might be good enough to get university scholarships, play in the WHL or even the NHL. Our telephone lines are open," said the radio host. "Let's talk about it . . ."

"Maybe one day you will make the Mustangs' Junior A team," said Dad. "Get a scholarship and play in the NHL."

Wow! thought Tom. *Dad dreams big.* Then he remembered: *That's my dream, too!*

———•———

The bright store buzzed with hockey players and parents shopping for gear. Tom and Dad checked out the skates on their way to the pants. "These will be next," said Dad. "You're growing like a weed!"

Tom tried on pants. The first pair was too padded. He looked like he had swallowed pillows. The next pair was too long. He couldn't bend his knees. The third pair was too big in the waist. They nearly fell to the floor as Tom stepped out of the change room.

Tom tried on the last pair. "This is it," he said.

"Walk around," suggested Dad. "Do some of your moves to make sure they're perfect. I'm going to find a helmet for me."

Tom sprang into action. He lunged, squatted, bent, reached and sat . . . next to a big guy wearing a Calgary Mustangs Junior A jacket. The name BAXTER was on his arm.

Wow! I'm sitting next to Butch Baxter! He is the best forward in the league! thought Tom, nearly jumping out of his new pants. *The radio announcer just said he's going to the WHL draft!*

Butch Baxter was busy taping his new hockey stick. He wrapped the white tape around and around the blade, while muttering the alphabet. "A, B, C, D, E . . ." Finally, he looked at Tom. "You getting some new hockey pants?"

"Yes. My old ones ripped," said Tom.

"Hope you got a goal when they ripped," said Butch.

"Nope," said Tom, nervously. His cheeks burned. How could he tell Butch Baxter that he didn't score goals? That his pants ripped in the dressing room?

"Oops. Sorry, dude," said Butch, looking at Tom's embarrassed face. "I only got a few

goals last season! Just didn't happen with
all the good goalies out there."

"But . . . but . . . you're the best forward," said
Tom, with admiration. "Everyone says that!"

"That's because I pass the puck and *assist*

the goals. I play as part of a team, not as a puck hog. Puck hogs are players who only go for goals. And when the other team figures it out, they go after *him*."

Tom listened hard.

Butch continued, "It takes more than one player to score. Everyone has a job on the ice. I try to line up the puck so that the best-positioned player can fire it into the net. Sometimes it's me, and sometimes it's not." Butch smiled. "And I'm lucky to have good defence behind me. They keep the puck away from our goal and feed it to me." Butch taped a few more loops. "I got the record for most assists last season: 105. And 5 assists in one game!" He pointed at Tom. "You get any assists yet?"

"Yeah . . . all the time. I already got seven assists this season, and we've only played six games!" said Tom.

"Good job. That's golden!" Butch gave Tom a thumbs-up.

Suddenly Tom felt like a million bucks. All along, he hadn't let his team down. And . . . he'd never known assists were *that* important.

Butch checked the time on his cellphone. "It's time to get to the arena. I *ALWAYS* tape my socks at exactly two hours and eight minutes before a game. That's when I get *into the zone* and give myself a pep talk."

"What zone?" Tom asked.

"My zone. It's when I concentrate and focus on my game. I get my mind prepared to play," said Butch. "Your *brain* and *body* need to be ready for a big game."

"Oh," squeaked Tom. He'd never thought of that either.

"Keep on passing!" said Butch. "Remember: a team wins together and loses together!"

"Okay, I'll keep passing," Tom assured Butch. But as Tom sat on the bench waiting for Dad, he had another thought. He crossed his fingers and said, "I'd like . . . just one more goal."

Lucky Tape

The house smelled like spicy spaghetti sauce. Tom put on his new hockey pants to show Mom.

"Nice," she said, turning him around. "Sturdy. Safe. Hey, what's this?" Mom peeled off a piece of stick tape stuck to Tom's backside. It was the length of a hot dog.

"Wowzers! That's from Butch Baxter! From when he taped his stick at the hockey store!" Tom hung the tape from his thumb. "It looks exactly like a . . . number 1!" Suddenly he had a mega idea.

Tom bolted to the mud room. His hockey bag sat open on the floor. He dug out his white home jersey. He put it on the floor, the large number on the back facing him. "Goodbye, number 5!" he said, sticking the number 1 beside the number 5. The white tape was almost invisible on the white jersey, but Tom knew it was there. "YES!" The piece of tape made his new jersey into an old secret weapon . . . number 15!

"Go, Hawks, go!" said Tom, as he pulled the jersey over his head. He ran to the backyard, grabbing his stick and a bucket of pucks on the way.

Old tires leaned against the brick wall. Tom used to be good at shooting pucks into the middle of the tires. He had done it hundreds of times. Now it was time to test his number 15.

Let's go! Tom fired a quick wrist shot,

hitting the target on his first try.

"Bull's eye!" Tom shouted. "I'm back!" He almost cried happy tears.

Tom fired shot after shot, hitting the target almost every time. Then he thought about

what Butch Baxter told him. *A great hockey player makes good passes. A team wins together and loses together.* Tom wondered how he could practise his passing.

Soon Tom had a new idea. He grabbed a tennis ball and hit it against the brick wall. The rebound was like a pass back to him. Tom picked up the ball on his stick, over and over, like a pass-receive drill. It wasn't perfect, but it felt great to keep the ball moving. When the ball was near the last target, Tom took a shot . . . and scored!

Mom came out of the house. "Tom, look at you! You have that hockey sweat head going on."

Tom glowed. Sweat head felt amazing!

"Now come inside for dinner. And *PEE-YEW!* Take off that smelly jersey. I'd better wash it for your game tomorrow," said Mom, rushing back to the kitchen.

Oh, no. Tom quivered. *Not number 15!* He took off the jersey and hid it inside his hockey helmet.

A rush of excitement tingled over Tom. Number 15 was going to surprise everyone!

Secret Luck

Wednesday.

Tom walked to school, still dreaming about hitting the tire targets in his backyard. He spied his friends and rushed to meet them. "Hey, guys! I'm here!"

"It's game day!" exclaimed Harty. "I've already checked my hockey gear."

"I'm ready, too!" said Jordan. He was wearing stinky socks.

Mark licked his lips. "I have Hawaiian pizza for recess snack and slapshot salami pizza for lunch."

Stuart looked worried. "I'm wearing my last NHL Band-Aid. Hope it doesn't fall off."

Tom whistled and hummed, nearly dancing an Irish jig. He had something lucky, too.

His friends raised their eyebrows at him. "What's going on?" they asked.

"Your smile is as big as a banana," said Mark.

Oh, no. Tom gulped. More than anything, he wanted to tell them about number 15 and how his luck was back. But Tom worried about bragging. If he shared his secret weapon, would it still be a secret? But mostly, would it still work?

Tom thought quickly, then said, "Coach Howie said we need a *positive* attitude. I am positive that we are going to have a good game!" He knocked his knuckles on his head and said, "Touch wood!"

"TOUCH WOOD!" they repeated, rapping heads.

The school day whizzed by. Tom doodled lucky 15s in every notebook.

———•———

It was exactly two hours and eight minutes before game time. Tom ate a bowl of hamburger soup. He checked his hockey bag. Everything was there.

"Where's Mom?" Tom asked.

"At work," answered Dad, without looking up from his laptop.

"But, it's game day!" said Tom. *What if we're late?* He remembered his "How to have bad hockey luck" and his "How to have good hockey luck" lists.

Tom checked the schedule. "Dad! Our game is at Crowfoot Arena. That's in Northwest Calgary."

Dad stopped. "Wow! That was lucky you checked. I assumed the game was at

Centennial Arena since you're the home team. I'd better phone Mom."

Tom and Dad hurried. They picked up Jordan and headed up Crowchild Trail to the arena. The car was quiet. Dad concentrated on the traffic. Tom and Jordan stared out the windows. They were concentrating, too.

Tom visualized himself skating down the ice, grabbing a pass and shooting it along the boards. He picked up the puck, passed and then positioned himself by the net. Should he shoot or pass?

"There's Mom," said Dad, pulling into the parking lot. She waved her yellow and green gloves.

"Our friends are here," said Tom, recognizing Mark's van. It had a Calgary Flames car flag sticking up from the window.

Coach Howie carried a first aid kit, coach's binder and a bucket of practice pucks up the stairs. He greeted the coach from the Falcons.

"Yeah! Let's go!" cheered Tom, ready to work hard for his team, the Hawks.

In the Zone

The dressing room rocked. The Hawks were *getting into the zone* with special routines. Everyone did something different. There was toe touching, knuckle cracking, hair combing, sock taping and music playing. Lucky charms sat on the bench: a superhero action figure, a lucky tape-ball, NHL playing cards, a bag of black rocks and a stuffed toy hawk.

Harty carefully put on his gear, paying attention to the lucky order. Elbow pads first, jock second . . .

Jordan's socks stank.

Mark patted his stomach, full of pizza.

Stuart wrote the letters NHL onto beige Band-Aids, using a black felt marker. He stuck them on his arm. "I've invented my own lucky Band-Aids," he said, "because I ran out of the real ones."

Tom suited up, saving the best for last. He slipped the number 15 jersey out of his bag without letting the team see the piece of stick tape. "Go, Hawks, go!" he said, poking his head through the neck hole.

Tom leaned back against the wall, making sure no one saw the tape. He felt the luck of 15 run up and down his back. A smile spread across his face. This was going to be his lucky day!

Coach Howie gave a quick pep talk. "Let's get out on the ice and play our best. We are not loony birds making nonsense plays . . . we are . . ."

"HAWKS!" shouted the team.

Tom fastened his helmet, sucked in a big breath of courage and thought, *Let's go, number 15.* He grabbed his stick, keeping his back close to the wall, and positioned himself at the end of the line.

The team filed out the door, along the mat and onto the ice. As Tom looked up into the stands, he could see his mom, dad, grandparents and all the Hawks' fans. They

were wearing yellow and green. Everyone cheered, "Go Hawks!"

"Break a leg!" shouted Harty's sister, Wendy.

"What?" Stuart panicked. "That's horrible! I don't want to break my leg!"

"Me neither," agreed Tom.

"It's a saying that means good luck. People say it before actors or dancers go on stage," said Harty, defending Wendy.

"How about we *break a sweat*?" said Tom. "We have five minutes to warm up."

Tom dug his blades into the ice and pushed off with long, smooth strides. He cruised by the players' bench and penalty box. *No penalties!* he reminded himself. He skated around the corners, doing perfect crossovers. He did a lap skating backwards, then stopped and joined a group taking shots on net.

Bang! Bang! Bang! Jordan stopped shot after shot. But he missed a five-hole, when Tom slid one through his open legs.

"Goal!" Tom squealed, losing his breath. "I got a goal!" He danced about like a guy with ants in his new hockey pants. *Number 15 is magic!* he told himself. Now his muscles were warm, and he was filled with confidence and luck!

Tom's friends started howling.

"Wow!"

"Wicked!"

"High-ten!"

"That's pizza perfect!"

The team gathered in front of their bench with Coach Howie, ready for their cheer. "Hawks!" they yelled, at the top of their lungs.

Tom skated to centre ice and set up for the faceoff . . . with a big smile on his face.

Game On

Plonk! The referee dropped the puck.

Tom swiped his stick, catching the puck and sending it to Mark on right wing. Mark skated along the boards and sailed the puck back to Tom. Tom skated hard to pick up the pass, but a Falcon barrelled ahead, grabbing the puck with his blade.

The Falcon raced down the ice, with Tom and Mark chasing after him. Stuart skated backwards, forcing the Falcon to the side, away from the goal. Jordan positioned himself and made his ugly goalie face.

Grrmph! The Falcon took a shot. He missed!

Stuart swooped in and grabbed the rebound. He quickly skated behind the net. He caught Tom's eyes and passed the puck right onto Tom's stick.

Tom skated up the middle of the ice. He passed to Mark. Mark returned the pass to Tom. Tom passed to Harty. Harty smacked the puck . . . right into the Falcons' net! GOAL!

"Yay!" shouted Tom, slapping high-fives with his friends.

"Yay!" screamed the players on the bench.

"Yay Hawks!" the fans cheered. They

waved their yellow and green flags.

Tom felt good skating to the bench. He heard the referee tell the scorekeepers, "Goal by number 8, assisted by number 5." Tom knew it was his number 15 bringing him good hockey luck. He watched the scoreboard post the goal: 1–0 for the Hawks.

A few minutes later, the Falcons had the puck. Their left winger skated around the Hawks and passed to an open player. She wound up at the blue line and pounded a slapshot right over Jordan's shoulder. GOAL! Now the score was 1–1.

"Rats," sighed Tom.

Jordan swigged back a drink of water. He shook his foot.

By the middle of the second period, the Hawks were in trouble. The score was 3–1 for the Falcons. The puck was in the Hawks' end. Tom felt sick inside.

"C'mon, 15. C'mon, 15." Tom begged for more luck. He stepped onto the ice to take the faceoff. "I can do it. I can do it."

Jordan scolded his skates as he stomped his feet. It looked like he was trying to wake up his stinky socks. As Tom skated by him, he said, "Hang in there, buddy!"

Jordan nodded and crouched into position.

"Go, Hawks, go! Go, Hawks, go!" chanted the fans.

Tom ignored the crowd. He ignored the score. He focused. The puck dropped.

Tom won the faceoff, making a slick pass to Mark. Mark skated down the ice. The puck zigzagged from Mark to Tom to Mark. Mark fired a shot. He scored!

"Yahoo!" hollered Tom.

"Yay!" cheered the fans.

"Yay!" The team banged their sticks on the boards.

The referee announced, "Goal by number 18, assisted by number 5."

Remembering what Butch Baxter said about assists made Tom glow.

The scoreboard read 3–2 for the Falcons.

The game continued at a fast pace. Coach Howie switched players on the ice every few minutes. He called for a time out.

"Keep up the good work, Hawks," Coach Howie told the team. "No penalties. A Falcons power play would kill us right now."

The clock dropped to two minutes remaining.

Stay strong! Tom told himself, stepping out of the players' box. He hustled to the action, jabbed his stick out and stole the puck. Tom dug his skates into the ice and got a breakaway! Nobody could catch him. Using a quick wrist shot, Tom fired the puck under the goalie's gloved hand. Goal!

"Yes!" Tom raised his arms and jumped about like an Irish dancer doing a sword dance.

His friends huddled around. "Woo-hoo!" they whooped and high-fived.

Excitement swirled inside Tom as he looked up into the stands. His parents waved like crazy. His Grandma Dot rang her cowbell. *Clang! Clang! Clang!*

"Yay!" shouted the crowd.

BUZZZ! The time clock sounded. The game was over. The final score was 3–3.

The Hawks and Falcons met on the ice to shake hands.

"Good game!" the Falcons' coach told Tom as he passed by him.

"Good game," agreed Tom.

Teamwork

The dressing room filled with sweat-head Hawks, all fired up.

"Two assists and one goal! Wowzers!" Tom zinged. He knew he couldn't have done it without lucky 15 on his back.

Tom peeled off his wet jersey. "What?" He panicked. The piece of tape from Butch Baxter was gone. *WHAT?? Oh, NO!* He couldn't believe his eyes. All he saw was the number 5!

Quickly, Tom searched the dressing room. As he walked toward the door, he saw the hot-dog length tape stuck to the wall.

There was only one time my back touched that wall, he remembered. *On the way out the door, BEFORE the game!*

Suddenly Tom had a brain flash, sparking like a red goal light. *Lucky 15 did NOT help me!* He staggered back to the bench in shock. *I played my best game this season with the worst luck . . . NUMBER 5!*

Coach Howie entered the dressing room carrying the game sheet. "Nice game, Hawks!" he hollered. He held up one hand.

They all sat up and listened.

"You worked hard out there," Coach Howie complimented them. "The game was fast. Our opposition was tough." He smiled. "We had no fluky goals. No penalties. No excuses. The passing was crisp. The shift changes were slick." He gave a thumbs-up. "You used your skills and your brains! Good comeback! Good job, HAWKS!"

"Yay!" the Hawks shouted.

Tom liked Coach Howie. It felt good to make him proud.

Mark called out, "It looks like a bird bath in here!" He shook his head, sprinkling his sweat outward.

The room exploded with laughter. Sweat was flying everywhere.

"I thought we were dead ducks when it was 3–1!" Mark continued. "But we kept pecking at that puck. Put two more eggs in the nest . . ."

"Yeah!" Everyone laughed along.

"And . . ." Mark motioned his friends to huddle together. He flicked his eyebrows and sang, "Tom's ALIVE . . . wearing number 5!"

"Yay, Tom!" Jordan waved a stinky sock in celebration.

Stuart shook his box of Band-Aids like a noisemaker. "Yippee!"

Harty gave Tom a high-ten. "That was top
shelf!"

"Thanks, guys," said Tom, smiling ear to
ear. "Teamwork got the goals and assists,
not just me!"

Mark chomped down on a piece of cold pizza. "So, you find a lucky charm yet? Spill the beans, man!"

"No!" crowed Tom. "Guess I should keep looking for my hockey luck."

"We'll help you," said Stuart. "Count on us!"

Tom stopped and thought: *TEAMWORK is my lucky charm! Getting goals is easier when we work together.*

"Let's hurry!" said Jordan. "The Flames game will be on the car radio!"

Tom proudly stuffed his number 5 jersey into his hockey bag. He smiled even more. *I*

am so lucky to have four best friends. They make everything fun! AND . . . together we make FIVE!

If you liked this book, look for these other books about Tom and his friends.

ISBN 978-0-439-94897-5

ISBN 978-0-545-99681-5

ISBN 978-0-545-99765-2

ISBN 978-1-4431-3345-6

ISBN 978 -1-4431-0442-5